# KOKOPELLI'S GIFT

Library of Congress Cataloging-in-Publication Data

Bryant, Kathleen.
  Kokopelli's gift / by Kathleen Bryant ; illustrated by Michelle Tsosie
Sisneros.
        p. cm.
  Summary: When a stranger named Kokopelli arrives at a drought-stricken
Puebloan village, he accepts gifts in exchange for teaching the
villagers to sing and dance to bring the rain.
  ISBN 1-885772-29-7
  1.  Pueblo Indians--Juvenile fiction. [1. Pueblo Indians--Fiction. 2.
Indians of North America--Southwest, New--Fiction. 3. Kokopelli (Pueblo
deity)--Fiction. 4. Gifts--Fiction.] I. Sisneros, Michelle Tsosie, ill.
II. Title.
  PZ7.B8394 Ko 2002
  [Fic]--dc21
                                        2002008591

Design by Rudy J. Ramos
Prepress by ALI Graphic Services Inc.
Printed in Hong Kong

9 8 7 6 5 4 3

Kiva Publishing
Walnut, CA

# KOKOPELLI'S GIFT

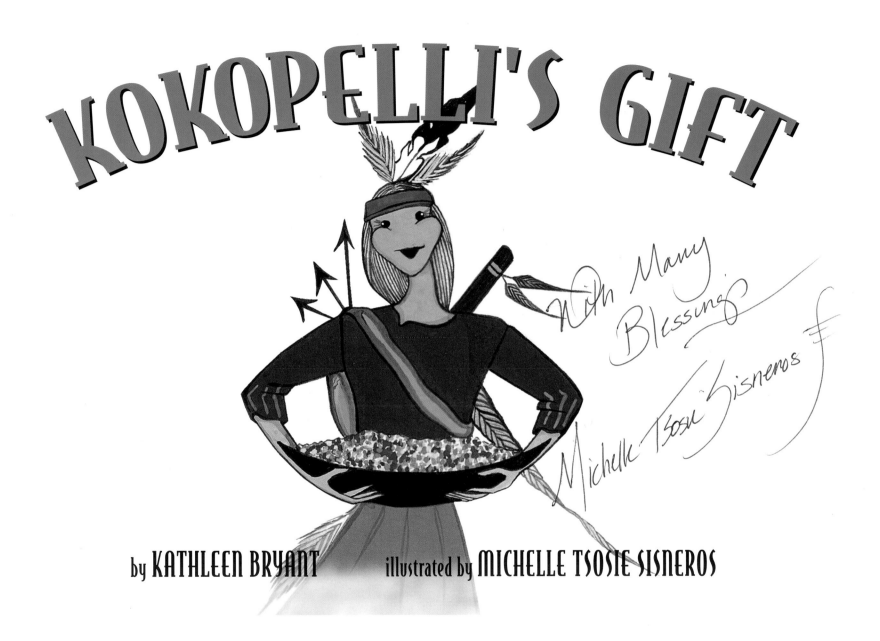

*With Many Blessings*

*Michelle Tsosie Sisneros*

by KATHLEEN BRYANT        illustrated by MICHELLE TSOSIE SISNEROS

KIVA
PUBLISHING, INC.

# Author's note

Kokopelli, the Fluteplayer, is one of the most recognizable figures in Southwestern art and culture. His image first appeared in Anasazi rock art two thousand years ago, and since then many peoples—including Hohokam, Pueblo, Navajo, and Apache—have depicted him in rock art, in pottery and jewelry designs, or as a kachina dancer.

Kokopelli has been called a god, a priest, a wandering trader, a trickster, and he has been connected with rain, growth, music, hunting, and magic. Sometimes Kokopelli is shown dancing or calling animals with his flute. In many pictures he appears to have a humped back. In some, he even looks like a bug or insect.

Was Kokopelli a real person or a legend or both? What was it about him that inspired people to draw his image and tell stories about him even to this day? We can't know for certain. But it is fun to wonder . . .

It was another hot summer day, and still the people worried that the rain might not come. Tempers were short, and only that morning mothers scolded children who strayed too far from the village, a cluster of stone structures set into a high alcove in the reddish sandstone cliffs. The granaries that held food for the coming winter were almost empty, and raiding parties were spotted near neighboring villages only days ago.

Nali sat on the plaza formed by the wide, mud-covered roof of the pueblo, twisting the long fibers of the yucca plant into a strong, thin rope used for making mats and sandals. Soon, when the strip of shade from the alcove's ceiling disappeared under the high afternoon sun, she could join the other children in play.

The liquid notes of a canyon wren echoed off the cliff walls above her. "Hello, Little Bird," she said softly. He visited nearly every morning and seemed to listen when she spoke to him.

"Do you know if the rains will come?" she asked him.

A breeze rustled the branches of a nearby juniper tree, and the wren flew away. She could see a traveler coming up the path to the village, carrying a pack on his back. He was tired and dirty and thin. Her fingers stopped working the fibers. She crept closer to the edge of the plaza and listened. The stranger asked the women grinding corn if he could speak to the village elders.

A young boy ran to the room where the elders gathered every morning. They came out and stood between the stranger and the village, murmuring to themselves. How had he walked past the young warriors who guarded the village granaries?

"My name is Kokopelli," he told them.

They looked him up and down. He was dressed in a simple cotton garment, a tattered feather headdress, and a pair of woven yucca sandals nearly worn through to the soles of his feet. Slung over his back was a sack made of animal skins.

"This stranger is a beggar," said one old man.

"A crazy man," said another.

"What if he is a thief, come to steal our grain?" asked a third.

The elders consulted together quietly, shaking their heads and pointing at the stranger. It was the custom to welcome travelers and share food, but these were hard times. At last one elder stepped forward.

"You may rest over there in the shade of the cliffs for awhile. Then be on your way."

The traveler left them and walked past
the village spring, seeping from a crack in the
side of the cliffs. Here, clusters of ferns grew bright
green against the red sandstone. The water dripped
so slowly that only a small, muddy puddle formed.
Below the spring, a large pot caught most of the
drips. Each drop was precious. He sat in the shade
of a juniper tree to rest. A canyon wren landed in
the branches nearby and began to sing.

He said a few words to the bird, then reached into his pack and took out his flute and started to play a song like the bird's. The sweet, clear notes climbed to the sky.

Nali heard the song that was like her friend the wren's, yet different. It was as though the stranger could speak to her wren in bird language. She set the yucca fibers aside, then climbed down the ladder through the roof and dashed out the door, following the sound until she came to the tree where the raggedy man sat.

She wasn't alone. The other children had followed the sound, too, and they formed a circle around the stranger. They stood and listened while he played on, marveling at how he could make his flute sound like a bird, or like the wind, or even like the water when it used to run from the spring and tumble over the rocks to a pool below. Happy sounds!

Soon the mothers wondered where their children were. They saw their footprints leading from the village to the cliffs and followed. They, too, heard the flute and stopped to listen. The circle around the juniper tree grew larger and larger, as more women and children arrived.

The stranger ended his next song on a high note that sounded like a hawk's cry. In the silence that followed, Nali dared to step forward and ask: "What do you carry in your pack?"

The stranger smiled. "Precious things, magical things. Would you like to trade?" Nali's mother reached down and pulled her back. "We have nothing," she said. "We traded all of our beautiful pots and weavings for food because our crops didn't grow."

"Will you play some more?" Nali asked.

"Ah, but my songs have value, too. Surely you must have something to trade. Show me what you have, for it is the gesture that matters."

Nali thought that someone who spoke to birds might like the same things she did. She reached into a small pouch tied around her waist.

"Here." She drew out her fist and opened it to reveal stones of many colors and shapes. "I found these where the stream used to flow."

The stranger reached out for the stones and held them up toward the bright sun. "Yes, these are special indeed. Gifts from the earth, shaped and polished by the water."

When they saw how pleased the stranger was, some of the women and children left the circle. They returned carrying things to trade, just in time to hear the end of a song about the stones and water. They sighed, because the notes of the song reminded them how water used to fall from the cliffs near the village after a rainstorm.

"And what do you bring?" the stranger asked a tall young boy, Nali's brother Poquay.

Poquay held out an arrow, its point shaped from glinting obsidian and its tail fletched with spotted feathers. "I'd like to hear another song," he said. "A prayer to make the game animals return to our canyon."

"Indeed. And your arrow will help carry the message to Sun Father."

As he played, others came forward with their gifts in exchange for songs: a small, blackened cooking pot, an orange-and-black feather, an assortment of bones. The stranger examined the gifts, telling them something about each one. "A pot is shaped from Mother Earth and filled with the breath of spirit, the power to make things live and grow. A feather carries our prayers to the gods."

Finally, one woman placed on the ground in front of the stranger a small handful of seeds. He stared at the seeds for a long time. "This is a very special gift, for I know these seeds are a gift of the future. They are the hope you have to make things grow and your faith that the rain will fall again. They are food. They are life. You have made a great sacrifice."

He reached for his pack, and all the women and children who watched drew in their breath, making a sound like the wind in the trees. He opened the pack and took out a small covered pot. When he lifted the lid, they leaned closer to see. Inside the pot were hundreds of seeds, of all different colors, like a rainbow.

"When people forget how to ask for rain, the seeds will wait until they remember again," he told them, adding the woman's gift of seeds to the ones he already had. "These seeds are from many places, lands farther away than your dreams. As long as they travel with me, they will live forever. Now, would you like to see what else is in my pack?"

"Yes!" they cried.

He lifted the pack by the bottom and shook it. Out dropped a small brown toad and a large insect, a locust with wriggling antennae. They stared in disbelief. Was the stranger crazy, as the elders claimed?

"I thank you for the things you have given me in exchange. Now I will play the song of rain."

He lifted the flute to his lips and the notes sighed like a breeze. The women and children could almost hear the clouds gathering on the wind.

"Sing," he told them. They stared.

He blew into the flute again, and this time the locust joined in, playing its hind legs like two sticks rubbing together. The toad croaked. Some of the children giggled, but a few others dashed among the junipers, looking for sticks they could rub together to make rasping sounds like the locust. Nali gathered a handful of pebbles and shook them, making them rattle.

The stranger's flute soared above it all, like the wind gathering strength. When those who weren't playing sticks realized the wind was blowing harder, twisting the branches of the juniper, they, too, searched the canyon bottom for stones and sticks to add their sounds to the music. Some of the older women, who remembered the right words, sang to Sun Father, asking him to make way for the Cloud Children.

The stranger played louder, leaping to his feet and springing around like the toad. "Dance!" he commanded. "Make your footsteps pound the earth like raindrops!"

They danced, women and children alike, and he played even louder. Their footsteps pattered over the ground, keeping rhythm with the banging stones and clattering sticks. The flute howled like a fierce breeze, and Sister Wind began to whip at their clothing and hair.

The stranger lay down on his back, lifting his flute to the sky. The women and children looked up and saw clouds gather above the canyon's rim. The stranger played on, wriggling his legs like a baby, kicking them up, up toward the clouds.

They danced harder, and more women began to sing as they learned the words to the rain song:

Cloud children are playing,
Closer they come.
Dancing in circles,
A gift they bring.

Soon the men in the village began to wonder where the women and children were. They could hear voices and music carrying to them on the wind. They left two warriors to guard the storehouses of grain, but the rest followed the sounds of the music, which now echoed through the canyon, bouncing off the cliff walls.

When they came to the place where they had sent the stranger, they saw all the women and children of the village singing and dancing with abandon.

"Join us," the women and children cried. "We are making rain."

The men began to dance, awkwardly at first. Then they, too, got into the spirit of the music. Several men ran back to the village, returning with drums and rattles. Sweat ran down the dancers' foreheads and dropped to the ground, and yet they danced on.

Then the loud voices of the Thunder People boomed above the singers. Some of the children cried in fright or in excitement, but they kept dancing. Nali felt a thrill of joy run through her down to the soles of her feet. The cracking thunder and howling wind nearly drowned out the music, so they sang louder.

"It's raining!" Poquay shouted. The dancers slowed their steps, lifting their hands toward the clouds to catch the rain on their palms.

The young boy was right. It was raining. The people laughed in joy as the raindrops pounded the earth.

"Where's Kokopelli?" Nali asked.

"Yes, where? We must have a feast to celebrate. He will be the guest of honor," said one of the elders.

They looked and looked, but the stranger was gone.

"Listen!" cried Poquay.

As the wind gusted toward them, they could hear the faint notes of a flute. The sound faded, and soon all they could hear was water singing down the sides of the cliff and tumbling into the pools below.

## About the Author

KATHLEEN BRYANT has written five novels and numerous magazine articles for *Arizona Highways, Sedona Magazine,* and other publications. *Kokopelli's Gift* is her first children's book, born out of her curiosity about fluteplayer legends and rock art imagery. The story's setting was inspired by a hot summer afternoon at Palatki, an ancestral pueblo built into the red sandstone cliffs of Sedona, Arizona.

Photo by Larry Lindahl

Bryant volunteers as an interpreter and site steward for the Red Rock Ranger District of the U.S. Forest Service and is a member of the Arizona Archaeological Society. She enjoys learning about the natural life and human history of the Southwest, especially when it involves hiking boots and a backpack.

## About the Illustrator

"The images I paint are from the people who touch my life in a profound way and the Mother Earth I live on." Grandniece of Pablita Velarde and niece of Helen Hardin, MICHELLE TSOSIE SISNEROS follows a legacy of notable Santa Clara Pueblo painters. She began painting as a child, and developed that into a full time painting career.

Photo by Murphy Sisneros

She has won numerous awards and honors for her paintings, including awards at Santa Fe Indian Market, the Gallup Ceremonial, and the Sundance Festival. *Kokopelli's Gift* is her first illustrated children's book.